Gandy and The Lady

Gandy
and the
Lady

First Printing: 2018

Artwork by Stephanie Lumayno

Telephone: 587-783-0059
Email: aamardon@yahoo.ca
Website: www.goldenmeteoritepress.com

Additional copies can be ordered from:
#103 11919-82 Street NW
Edmonton AB
T5B 2W4
CANADA

ISBN 978-1-77369-013-1 (paperback)

My name is Gandy. I'm a Basset Hound. I live with Barney. He's a Geographer. Most of the year he teaches at our University. During breaks we go on lots of adventures together. This year he's not going to teach. He's on sabbatical. That's something teachers take that is kind of like a vacation, but it's to study something to become better teachers.

Barney is taking his Sabbatical in Poland.
He is helping researchers find things that
are buried under the ground by looking
at special pictures taken from space by
satellites. He is helping them map places
that were used for bad things during
World War II. Barney uses a drone with
camera and GPS tracker.

That was a war that started in Europe
in 1939. Poland was occupied by Nazi
Germany on one side and the Soviet
Union on the other. Lots of bad things
happened to the Polish people. Bad things
always happen in war, but these were
especially bad.

It wasn't just soldiers who got killed, but lots of women and children too, especially Jewish people. All of their evil was because of hate. They didn't hate people because of something they had done. They hated people just because of who they were. They hated their color or their religion. The Nazis tried to hide the evil they were doing by doing a lot of it in Poland. Both the Nazis and the Soviets tried to hide what they had done by burying it.

Barney told me that it's very important to remember the people who were hurt and killed so that we never let it happen again. Most of the witnesses who saw what happened are gone or really old. He's in Poland to help dig up the buried places so they can speak for the witnesses after they are all gone. It's important for us to teach everyone how important it is to not hate. Hate makes me sad.

Today we have been mapping in a forest called Katyn. This is a place where the Soviets buried Polish people they killed. They wanted to make Poland a part of the Soviet Union, so they wanted to get rid of the Polish leaders, teachers, military officers, and priests who might oppose them.

Barney has been trying to find spots in the forest for archeologists to dig. They are trying to find people who have been lost so their families can know what happened to them. He uses a really nice GPS tracker on his drone to fly in between the trees but above the underbrush. That way he can find spots identified from the satellite pictures even if they are buried under lots of bushes and trees.

Sometimes we play hide and seek.
Barney puts the tracker on my harness,
and I hide in the woods. He finds me with
the drone and sneaks up on me. Once
I hid in a hollowed out log, but he still
found me.

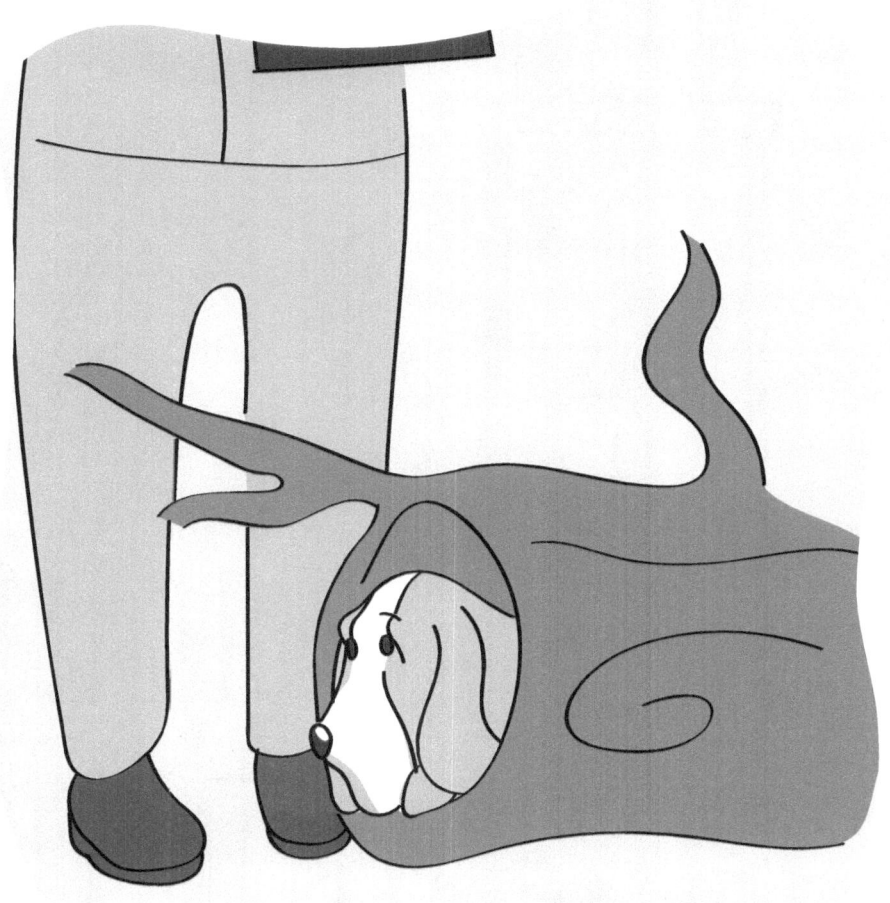

On the weekends, Barney and I have been
visiting different cities in Poland.
We've seen the castle in Krakow,

A big church in Licheń Stary,

We even went to see a house in Szymbark that was built upside down. It didn't have a dog door.

We went to see a special church in Czestochowa to see a special painting that is called an icon. That's a painting of a holy person that reminds us to try to be holy ourselves. This icon is called Our Lady of Czestochowa, or sometimes the Black Madonna because it is so old that centuries of candle smoke have darkened the image.

We went during the feast day in August, and there were lots of pilgrims both in the streets and the church. Pilgrims are people who take special trips to visit religious places. We brought along the drone, because Barney likes to get pictures of the places we visit from the air.

Lots of the people on the street looked up at the drone and waved. While we were taking pictures, we heard screams coming from the church. Someone ran past us into the street carrying the Icon.

He ran past us and disappeared into the crowd. One of the monks ran outside onto the steps screaming that someone had stolen the Lady. Barney looked at me and said, "Gandy, find him. I'll follow you with the drone."

I put my nose to the ground, and began running through the legs of everyone in the crowd lining the street in front of the church. I kept running and running as the scent of the man got stronger in my nose. Then I found him, and he was sprawled half in the street and half on the sidewalk. The icon was lying on the sidewalk next to him quite safe. It looked as if he had tripped on the curb, and when he fell down, he had stabbed himself on a post.

I heard the drone overhead, and knew
that Barney would know where I was. I
stood by him until Barney and two of the
monks found us. Every time he looked like
he was going to try to get up, I growled
to keep him on the ground. He was really
too hurt to try to escape. One of the
monks picked up the icon and said, "Our
Lady is preserved." The other monk said,
"She has always been able to take care of
herself."

The police arrived and then an ambulance crew to take the thief away. The monks thanked us for our help. Barney put the drone back in its case, and we walked back to the train station to take us back to our hotel in Krakow. He said, "Gandy man, we sure have had an adventure."

The End.